D0962338

My dentist is not a monster /
E MOF   2039571

Moffatt, Julia.
Granby Elementary School

My Dentist Is Not a Monster

ISBN 0-7696-4030-3

50395

EAN

9 780769 640303

School Specialty
Children's Publishing

Text Copyright © Evans Brothers Ltd. 2004. Illustration Copyright © Anni
Axworthy 2004. First published by Evans Brothers Limited, 2A Portman
Mansions, Chiltern Street, London W1U 6NR , United Kingdom. This edition
published under license from Zero to Ten Limited. All rights reserved. Printed in
China. This edition published in 2005 by Gingham Dog Press, an imprint of
School Specialty Children's Publishing, a member of the School Specialty Family.

Library of Congress-in-Publication Data is on file with the publisher.

Send all inquires to:
8720 Orion Place
Columbus, OH 43240-2111

ISBN 0-7696-4030-3

1 2 3 4 5 6 7 8 9 10 EVN 10 09 08 07 06 05 04

My Dentist Is Not a Monster

By Julia Moffatt

Illustrated by Anni Axworthy

GINGHAM DOG PRESS

Columbus, Ohio

Today was Danny's first trip to the dentist.

Danny did not want to go.

His brother had told him about it.

His brother said the dentist was scary.
He said the dentist was a big monster.

He lived in a cave and carried a
sharp drill.

Danny never, ever wanted to go to the dentist.

He hid under his bed.

But his mother found him.

"You have to go to the dentist,"
she said.

"The dentist keeps your teeth clean and healthy," Mom explained.

15

Danny still did not want to go. "Come on, Danny. It will be okay," said Mom.

Inside, Danny was surprised.

It did not look like a scary cave.

The dentist did not look like a monster.

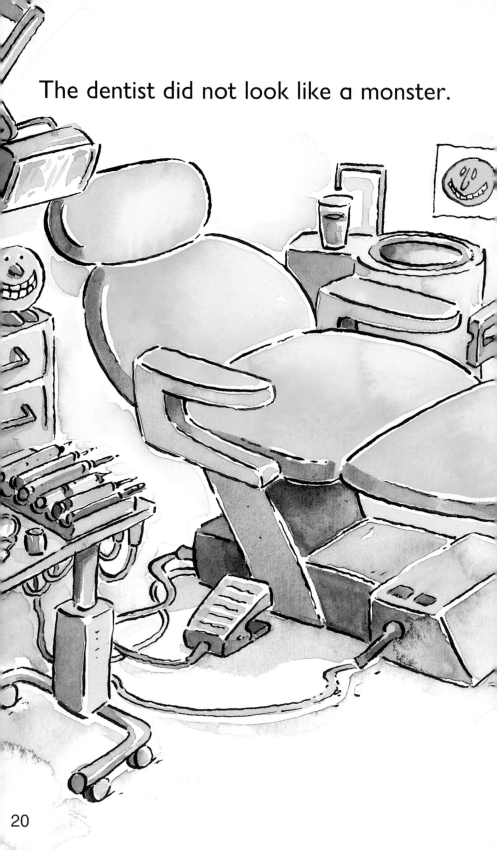

"Would you like a ride in my chair?"
he asked.

"Sure," said Danny. "Whee!"

"Open wide," said the dentist.

The dentist cleaned Danny's teeth.
Then, he told Danny to brush his teeth
two times a day.

He even gave Danny a sticker.

29

"This is fun!" said Danny.
"My dentist is not a monster after all."

Words I Know

about	not
clean	said
come	today
have	want

Think About It!

1. Why didn't Danny want to go to the dentist?
2. How did Danny's brother describe the dentist?
3. Describe what the dentist in the story was really like.
4. How did Danny's feelings about the dentist change at the end of the story?

The Story and You

1. Have you ever been afraid of something that turned out to be okay?
2. Describe your last trip to the dentist. Were you scared?
3. What do you think would happen to your teeth if you never visited the dentist?